Today Keith is going to play games with his Super Stunt Rally Racer.

It has lots of special features.

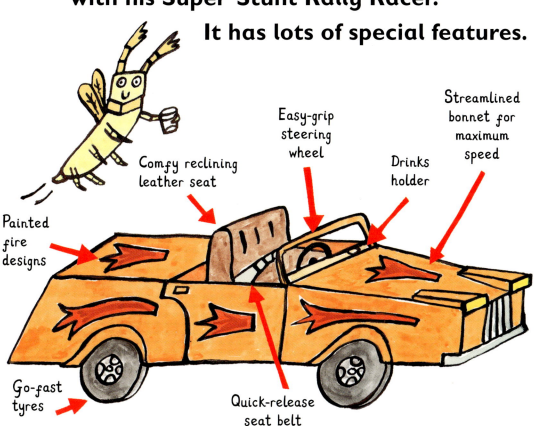

Easy-grip steering wheel

Streamlined bonnet for maximum speed

Comfy reclining leather seat

Drinks holder

Painted fire designs

Go-fast tyres

Quick-release seat belt

Stunt Jumping

Keith is an excellent Stunt Jumper.
Here he is zooming down the road
at maximum speed.

over
Jo-Jo in her
Row-and-Go Boat ...

over
Stacie on her
Penny Farthing ...

over the
Triplets in their
Space Rocket ...

"Excellent, Keith!"

"You can do it, Keith!"

"Go!"
"Go!"
"Go!"

Fast Driving

Keith is giving Mr Thornton-Jones and friends a ride in his Super Stunt Rally Racer. Everyone loves it when Keith drives really, really fast!

Fly Drive

Now Keith is going to attempt to Fly Drive over Pauline and the girls in their Mud Truck, while giving a lift to lots of friends.

"Come on, Keith!"

"Hey, the car feels very heavy!"

Pauline and the girls have seen Keith try to Fly Drive before.

"Come on, Tate, you can do it!"

"Go, Giorgio!"

Tate's Rally Car has lots of stickers on it.

Giorgio has added extra wheels and caterpillar tracks to his Rally Car.

Vroom!
Vroom!

Whoops! Keith and Tate are
slipping all over the place on
this muddy patch of road.

Bye-bye, Keith

Keith has had great fun with his Super Stunt Rally Racer and now he is very tired. Keith has had a glass of nice warm milk and reclined his comfy leather seat. Here he is having a little snooze.